NICK BUTTERWORTH AND MICK INKPEN

THE MOUSE'S TALE

Sometimes, grown-ups find it hard to believe in miracles. In Nick Butterworth and Mick Inkpen's delightful *Animal Tales*, special occasions in Jesus' life are seen through the eyes of some of God's smaller creatures, who have no trouble at all understanding exactly what is happening...

Marshall Pickering is an Imprint of
HarperCollins*Religious*
Part of HarperCollins*Publishers*
77-85 Fulham Palace Road, London W6 8JB

First published in Great Britain
in 1988 by Marshall Pickering

This edition published in 1994

Text and illustrations Copyright © 1988
Nick Butterworth and Mick Inkpen

The authors and illustrators each assert the moral right to be
identified as the authors and illustrators of this work

A catalogue record for this book is
available from the British Library

ISBN 0 551 02875-0

Printed and bound in Hong Kong

Co-edition arranged by Angus Hudson Ltd, London

NICK BUTTERWORTH AND MICK INKPEN

THE MOUSE'S TALE

JESUS AND THE STORM

Hello, I'm a mouse, a ship's mouse. And this is my house. It's a fishing boat.

In the evening, when the fishermen have gone home, that's when I wake up. I come out and sniff and nibble the fishing nets.

Well, the other evening, a strange thing happened.

I'm nosing about on deck as usual when suddenly, there's a noise. Quick as a flash I hide behind some old ropes.

Listen, there are footsteps! The fishermen have come back. Twitch my whiskers and sniff the air. There's someone with them.

I can hear the fishermen untying the boat. Splish splash. I can feel them pushing it out into the waves. The wind catches the sail, the mast creaks, the boat rocks gently and we're heading out to sea.

'It's been a long day,' says a voice I don't know. 'I think I'll get some sleep.'

Where are we going? We're not going fishing. It's too late for fishing. Where are we going?

We're taking the man with the voice I don't know for a ride in our boat.

The man sits down right next to me and leans his head on my ropes. His hair smells warm. He's not a fisherman.

Everything is quiet except for the waves slapping under the boat.

Soon the man is asleep. I want a better look at him. I creep out from under the ropes. All clear.

The man looks very tired. He has a kind face and he snores.

His breath tickles my whiskers. He can ride in our boat if he likes. I wonder what his name is.

All of a sudden – Flash! Bang! I'm off and running.

Flash! Bang! Lightning and thunder! I scamper up the deck and down my hole.

Flash! Bang! We're in for a rough ride. These summer storms can be nasty.

Now the great black clouds close in.
The sky grows dark.

Big drops of rain begin to splatter on
the deck. The sail flaps and bangs and
gulps the wind.

The storm whips spray across the
deck and giant waves slam the boat.

The boat begins to roll and slide.

One moment up, next moment down. Up and down, up and down with water crashing on the deck and pouring on my head.

And all the while – Flash! Bang! Lightning and thunder. And all the while – Slap! Crack! The wind tatters our sail. And all the while the man sleeps on ... and snores.

'Wake up! Wake up! We're going to sink! Wake up! Wake up! We'll all be drowned! Wake up! Wake up! We're going down! Jesus, wake up!'

So that's his name.

Slowly, the man opens his eyes. He blinks and rubs his face and looks around.

And holding on the mast, he stands up straight.

Then stretching out his hand he shouts into the wind.

His voice is firm and strong and very, very loud.

'Peace!' he shouts. 'Be still!'

And straight away the storm does what he tells it to!

The wind dies down, the thunder stops, the sea is calm and all is still.

Can you believe it? The wind, the lightning, thunder, waves and rain all stop! What kind of man is that?

The setting sun peeps out behind a cloud. The men get out the oars to row us home. I shake the water from my paws and ears and settle down to sleep.

So pull the oars, we'll soon be home to tell the tale.

And that man Jesus, if he wants to, he can sail with us again.

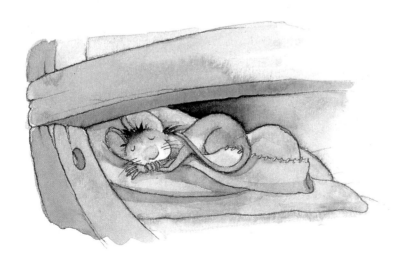

If you enjoyed this *Animal Tale*,
you can also read

The Cat's Tale – Jesus at the Wedding
The Fox's Tale – Jesus is Born
The Magpie's Tale – Jesus and Zacchaeus